The Feather-Bed Journey

Paula Kurzband Feder
Illustrated by Stacey Schuett

ALBERT WHITMAN & COMPANY • MORTON GROVE, ILLINOIS

To Karen and Corin Hewitt
and in memory of Frank Hewitt.
P.K.F.

In memory of my great-grandmother Mutz
and my grandmothers, Gammy and Nana.
S.S.

Library of Congress Cataloging-in-Publication Data

Feder, Paula Kurzband.
  The feather-bed journey / written by Paula K. Feder;
illustrated by Stacey Schuett.
     p.   cm.
Summary: As she rescues the insides of a torn feather pillow,
Grandma tells about her childhood in Poland, about the Nazi
persecution of Jews during World War II, and about the
origin of this special pillow.
  ISBN 0-8075-2330-5
  1. Jews—Poland—Juvenile fiction. [1. Jews—Poland—
Fiction. 2. Grandmothers—Fiction. 3. Holocaust, Jewish
(1939-1945)—Fiction. 4. Pillows—Fiction.] I. Schuett, Stacey,
ill. II. Title.
  PZ7.F3113Fe   1995   95-3123
  [E]—dc20   CIP
                                                      AC

Text copyright © 1995 by Paula Kurzband Feder.
Illustrations copyright © 1995 by Stacey Schuett.
Published in 1995 by Albert Whitman & Company,
6340 Oakton Street, Morton Grove, Illinois 60053-2723.
Published simultaneously in Canada
by General Publishing, Limited, Toronto.
Printed in the United States of America.
10 9 8 7 6 5 4 3 2 1

Designer: Karen Johnson Campbell.
Text typeface: Trump Mediaeval.
Illustration media: Acrylic and pastel.

Rachel's grandmother had a soft, warm feather pillow. Sometimes she would let Rachel sleep with it. The pillow went "woomph" when Rachel laid her head on it. Every Passover Seder, Grandpa would sit at the head of the table and rest against the pillow. Sometimes Grandma would hug the pillow with a faraway look in her eyes.

Early one windy evening, Rachel's little brother, Lewis, came into her room. The windows were open. Rachel was punching the pillow. Smack, whack, thwack!

"What are you doing?" asked Lewis.

"Grandma said feather pillows need lots of fresh air and exercise."

"Let *me* exercise it," said Lewis, and he grabbed the pillow.

"Give it back to me!" said Rachel.

"No! I have it now." Lewis ran downstairs.

Rachel followed him down the stairs, past their mother and father, past Grandma and Grandpa, and out the door.

"Oh, dear! Lewis has the pillow," said Grandma. She ran to the door. "Come back!" she cried. "Bring the pillow back!"

In the coming darkness, Rachel pulled at the pillow, and Lewis held on tight. Suddenly it tore. Soft little white feathers flew up in the air.

"Oy, oy! No, no, no!" cried Grandma, and she ran out of the house. "Rachel, Lewis. Catch the feathers! We must save them all."

Grandpa came outside. He picked up the torn pillow. "Here," he said. "We can put the feathers back in. Hurry!"

The wind blew the feathers up and down and around and around.

Lewis jumped up again and again, catching feathers as they flew near him.

Mom and Dad ran across the street and picked up feathers from a neighbor's lawn.

The wind blew many feathers far away. The street lights went on. A few feathers floated past the yellow lights.

Grandma sighed. "No more," she said. "It's too dark. This will have to do. Oh, I wish I could find them all!"

Grandpa put his arm around Grandma. "Remember," he said, "it's a very special pillow. We can sew it up. It's okay for it to get smaller."

"Why can it get smaller?" asked Lewis.

"Why is it special?" asked Rachel.

"Once it was a feather bed," said Grandma.

"A feather bed?" said Lewis. "How can you sleep on such a little bed?"

"Once upon a time, it wasn't little," said Grandma.

"Tell me the once-upon-a-time story, Grandma," said Rachel. "The feather-bed story."

"This is the feather-bed story," said Grandma. "A long time ago, I lived with my mother and father in a small town in faraway Poland. I had two older sisters, but they were married and lived in another town. My mother made the feather bed. Her name was Freydl Rockovitsky."

"She was my great-grandmother," said Lewis.

"Don't interrupt," said Rachel.

Grandma went on. "When I was a little girl," she said, "I slept on that feather bed. Or, if it was very cold, I slept under it. It was filled with soft goose down. We had our own geese, and we plucked their down."

"That wasn't nice," said Lewis. "It hurt the geese."

"They were loose feathers, Lewis. They were easy to pull off."

"Easy to pull off, but not so easy to get!" said Grandpa.

"No," said Grandma. "First my mother had to catch the goose. She would put it in her lap and hold its head between her knees. Then she'd pick the soft, downy feathers from its neck and breast. Flicken, we called it in Yiddish. Pulling feathers. The goose would pull loose sometimes and pinch Mama's arms. It wouldn't let go. Oh, she would be black and blue for many days."

"How many feathers did she get?" asked Lewis.

"It took many to fill up a feather bed. A thousand million, Mama would say. And when it was filled high with those feathers, it was finished. Then Mama would sew the covers up and sew her initials, in Yiddish, on a corner.

"On nice days, Mama would shake it out and give it some sun and fresh air. It got so puffy I thought it was at least ten feet high. Then I would run and jump right in the middle of it. It would go 'woomph,' like air shooting out of a balloon."

"Just like our pillow," said Rachel.

"Now tell how it became a pillow," said Lewis.

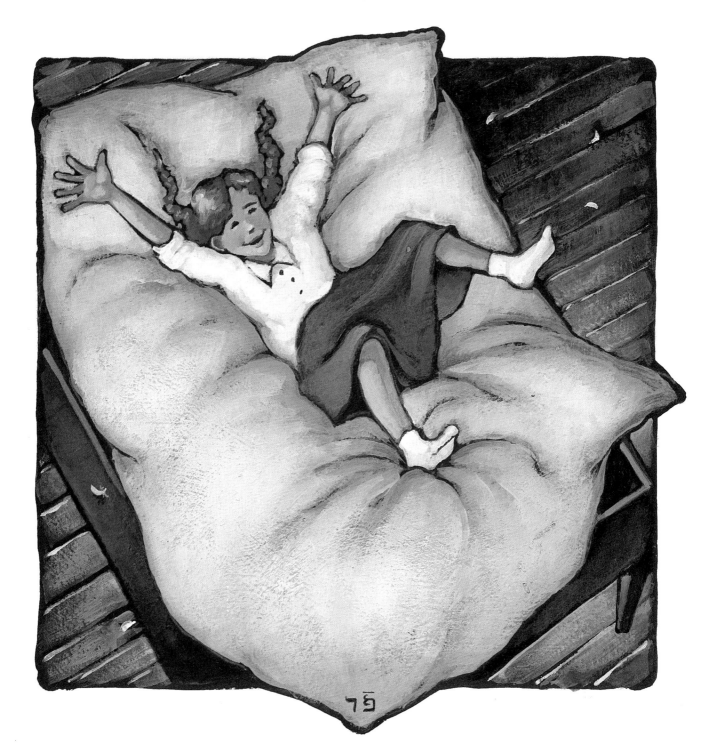

Grandma took a breath and let it out slowly. "Sad times came to us," she said. "War began. Certain people from Germany, called Nazis, came to Poland. They didn't want Jews in Poland. They didn't want Jews anywhere.

"They made Jewish people sew a yellow star on their clothes. They beat up Jews. They killed them just because they were Jews.

"And," said Grandma, "my papa was told not to go to his job anymore. We couldn't travel, and I wasn't even allowed to go to my school."

"Oh, Grandma," said Rachel, and she held her grandmother's hand.

"One terrible day, they made us get out of our house. We didn't have time to take much.

"They drove us to an old part of a big city. It was called a ghetto. Only Jews lived there now, and they had built a wall around it.

"It was so crowded! Two families lived with us in one room.

"It was a cold winter that year, and there was very little food. I was always hungry. My stomach hurt so much."

"I hope you took your feather bed," said Rachel.

"Yes, and that was what kept us children warm. Six children shared that feather bed."

"Then what happened?" asked Lewis.

"Things got worse and worse. People were dying of hunger and sickness. Sometimes Nazis came and took people away. We never saw them again."

"But *you* didn't die, Grandma," said Rachel. "You were lucky."

"Why were you lucky?" asked Lewis.

"Because I got out of the ghetto," said Grandma. "Mama and Papa stayed behind. It was safer for only one person to escape. They said I had my whole life to live still. I was your age, Lewis—seven years old.

"I was scared and I didn't want to leave Mama and Papa. But Papa had a plan. He knew of a Christian farmer who might help hide me. Papa sent a secret message to this farmer and promised him some money. The farmer sent a message back.

"Two nights later, with the money in my hand, I sneaked through a hole in the ghetto wall. It was cold; I missed Mama and Papa already. I was afraid I might never see them again.

"The farmer's name was Jan Witkowski. He met me and took me to his house. He and his family hid me and used the money to buy food for me.

"I hid in a secret compartment in the basement. There I stayed most of the time. I could never go outside or even look out a window because the neighbors might see me and wonder. A few times Nazi soldiers came to the house to look for hidden Jews. I was so scared! I could hear their big boots walking on the floor above me."

"Ooh, but that was scary! What did you eat?" asked Rachel.

"Cabbage and cabbage and cabbage. Sometimes some noodles. And I slept on a pillow filled with dried peas."

"Dried peas!" squealed Lewis. He put his hand over his mouth to keep from laughing.

"It's not funny," said Rachel. "I'm glad I have my feather pillow, Grandma."

"Feather pillow! Feather bed!" shouted Lewis. "What happened to the feather bed? Did you take it with you?"

"No. Mama and Papa and other people who stayed in the ghetto needed it."

"Then my feather pillow can't be from your feather bed," said Rachel.

"It certainly is," said Grandma, "and I'll tell you why. I stayed with Mr. Witkowski for two years, but one day, a neighbor began to ask questions. She had seen me do something I shouldn't have done. I peeked out a window. If she were to tell the Nazis, they would kill me and the Witkowski family, too.

"The next night, Mr. Witkowski sent me into the woods. He let some people who were hiding there know. I hid with those people for two more years.

"Other brave men and women sent us food and found us shelter. Sometimes we ate. Sometimes we didn't. I wish more people had been as kind and as brave.

"One day, at last, the war was over," continued Grandma. "All of us came out of the woods. We were sent to a camp filled with people who had escaped the Nazis. At that camp, I found my mother, but I never saw my father or my sisters again. They had all been killed.

"Finally after six months, we were allowed to go to America. We were safe at last."

Everyone was quiet for a minute. Then Rachel asked, "What about the feather bed, Grandma?"

Grandma smiled. "After we were settled in America," she said, "Mama wrote to Jan Witkowski to thank him for saving my life. We didn't even know if he was still alive.

"But one day, the last day of Hanukkah, when our neighbors were there to celebrate, the postman came to our house.

He had a big package. It had come all the way from Poland."

"A Hanukkah present!" said Lewis.

"The feather bed!" yelled Rachel.

"Well, let me tell you. It was, and it wasn't."

"That's a riddle," said Rachel. "What was it, Grandma?"

"Shh—I said I would tell you. Inside the package was a pillow, and on the pillow was a letter. It was from Mr. Witkowski. He told us he had helped others, too. Someone gave him the feather bed to thank him. They told him it had belonged to my mother."

"Finish the riddle," said Rachel.

"Ah—the answer to the riddle," said Grandma. "This is what else he wrote. I remember every word."

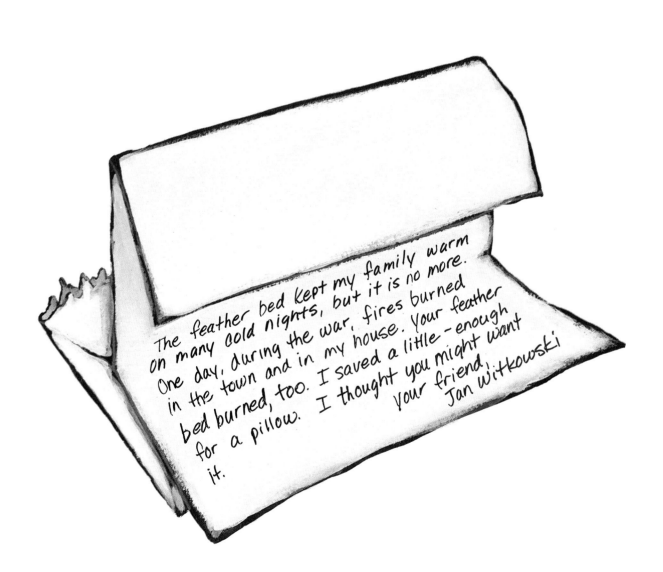

The feather bed kept my family warm on many cold nights, but it is no more. One day, during the war, fires burned in the town and in my house. Your feather bed burned, too. I saved a little—enough for a pillow. I thought you might want it.

Your friend,
Jan Witkowski

"And that's the answer to the riddle," said Rachel. "The feather bed turned into a pillow."

"Grandma, how did you know it was your feather bed?" asked Lewis.

Grandma carefully picked up the torn pillow. There on a corner were the initials of Grandma's mama.

A few feathers floated up in the air. Grandma caught them.

"It's going to be a little pillow now," said Rachel.

"But always a very special pillow," said Grandma. "And now you know why."

Before World War II, 10 percent of Poland's population was Jewish. When the Germans occupied Poland in 1939, they severely limited the freedom of the Jews. Anti-Jewish decrees made life unbearable. There had always been a history of anti-Semitism in Poland, but treatment of Jews became much worse during the occupation.

In 1940, Jews were placed in ghettos. Although people tried to live as normally as possible, crowding produced starvation and disease. Many died. Some rebelled. Some escaped, but the majority were sent to concentration camps. There few survived, and few Jews are left in Poland today.

The Nazis also persecuted Gypsies, homosexuals, Communists, Jehovah's Witnesses, the disabled, and the mentally ill.

During the war, some sympathetic Poles hid Jewish children at the risk of their own lives. They hid them in basements, attics, convents, orphanages, haylofts, and secret compartments. The children had to learn to deny their names and religion. All were deprived of their childhoods.

Today's children must learn about history, even when history is about evil. Perhaps the best way is to tell a particular story and, in telling, help children to think about what it must have been like to be cold, hungry, afraid, and separated from one's mother and father.

We can talk to our children about prejudice and its results. We can point out the devastation of war. Perhaps most important, we can talk about courage and acts of goodness in the midst of horror.

Then it will be our children, armed with an understanding of the past, who can stand up and say, Never again.

Paula K. Feder